Sven Nordqvist

MERRY CHRISTMAS,
Festus and Mercury

Carolrhoda Books, Inc.
Minneapolis

For two days, Festus and Mercury had stayed indoors watching the snow fall. Finally, on the morning before Christmas Eve, the sky was clear. Festus was anxious to go to the store to buy groceries. There was hardly a scrap of food in the house, and there was so much to do to get ready for Christmas.

Mercury the cat had rummaged through the cupboard to find the Christmas tree stand and was waiting with his nose pressed against the door.

"Festus!" the cat called. "Come on, let's go and chop down a Christmas tree!"

"We'll have to do that after we go to the store," said Festus. "But first, I'd better clear away some of that snow."

They went outside and Festus cleared paths to the hen house, the workshop, the outhouse, and the woodshed.

"As long as we're out here, we ought to collect some fir branches for the front door," said the old man. "Do you want to come along, Mercury?"

"Well, of course I want to come along!" exclaimed the cat.

As Festus climbed up the hill, he cut branches and Mercury piled them onto the sled. When the sled was full, they started back toward home. All of a sudden, Festus slipped and the sled flew forward, knocking the old man right on top of the fir branches. The next thing he knew, he was speeding out of control down the hill. A stone wall rose up in front of him and smash! The sled, the branches, and Festus tumbled into the snow.

The cat laughed and cheered, "Do that again!" But the old man did not look as if he thought it were funny at all. He moaned and groaned as he struggled to his feet.

"Oh, rats," he flinched. "I've really done it this time. I can't stand on my foot."

Mercury stopped laughing and tried to think of something helpful to say, but he couldn't.

Festus managed to limp home, where he sat and examined his foot. "What rotten luck! I hope it gets better before the store closes, or we won't have any food for Christmas," he said.

"Oh, yes! We have to buy fish and ham and sausages," said Mercury eagerly. "Come on, we'd better go right now!"

"We'll have to wait until my foot is better," sighed Festus. "And there's still so much to do. Chop down a tree, scrub the kitchen floor..."

"I can do that!" said the cat, and he ran to the cupboard for the scrub brush and bucket.

"Well, I suppose you could," the old man said. "But, remember, you'll have to dry the place properly when you've finished!"

"Of course," promised Mercury.

Festus filled the bucket with soapy water and stretched out on the bench. He hardly had both his feet up before the water came rushing across the floor. Mercury had knocked over the bucket and was surfing across Kitchen Creek on the scrub brush. He balanced on one leg, then another, zigzagging around the furniture. Waves of water rolled across the kitchen and splashed into the back door.

After five minutes, Mercury was completely exhausted.

"I'm all finished," he gasped and sank onto a chair.

"Oh, no, that is exactly what you are not," Festus scolded. "You have to clean up after yourself this time, because I can't do it with this foot."

"But I'm too tired. After all, I'm just a tiny little cat," Mercury said pitifully.

"I'll try to feel sorry for you while you're doing it," said Festus. "And when you're through, we'll bake some gingerbread."

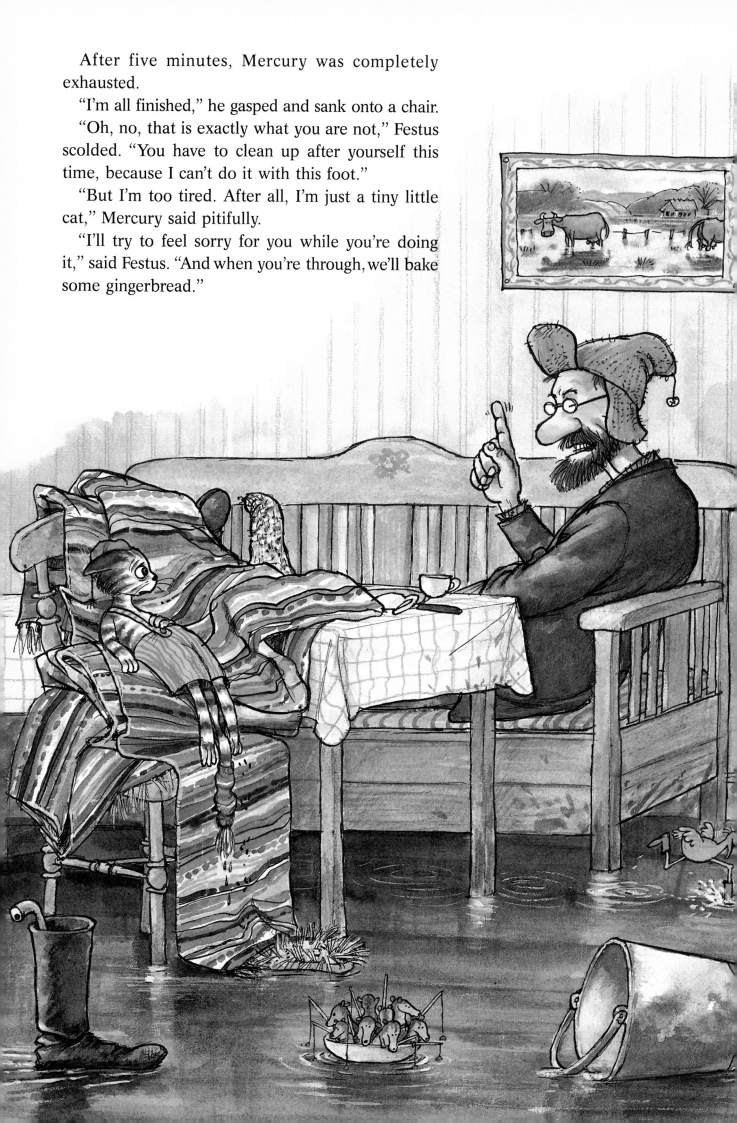

It was dusk when Mercury finished, and Festus had fallen asleep. Mercury shouted in his ear to wake him.

"Wake up, old man! We've got gingerbread to bake!"

Festus hobbled to the pantry to get the gingerbread dough left over from last week. But when he looked in the bowl, there was only a little lump left.

"It shrank," said Festus.

"Yes, funny thing about dough," said Mercury. "It just disappears."

"Maybe some cat has eaten it?" Festus asked.

"Maybe," said the cat. "Or some old man perhaps?"

"Perhaps," said the old man.

Festus rolled out the dough that was left anyway. Mercury cut out the shapes and ate the pieces in between.

Then they sat together drinking coffee, eating gingerbread, and staring into the darkened window. The house was silent and still as they each thought about Christmas and how it was turning out.

"The store is closed until after Christmas now. I guess we won't have any Christmas food," said Festus sadly. "We'll have to make do with what we've got—some carrots and a can of sardines."

"Carrots on Christmas Eve! Yuck!" spat Mercury.

"It's not *so* bad," said Festus. "At least you'll be getting a Christmas present."

"What is it?" the cat sulked.

"You'll see tomorrow," said Festus. "Now I'm going to wrap up this foot, and then I'm off to bed."

Festus wrapped his foot in two woolen socks, a sweater, and a pair of long johns, and tied it all up with a piece of string. Now the foot really looked sore. Then he went to sleep.

Mercury stewed awhile longer. Then he remembered there was one thing he could still do. He ran to the workshop to get the potato peeler he had found the other day. It might have been a lousy day-before-Christmas Eve, thought the cat, but at least the old man will get a present. And when he finished wrapping the present, Mercury felt a lot better.

The next morning, Festus's foot still hurt.

"I'm afraid we won't be able to cut down a Christmas tree," he said.

"WHAAAAT?" cried Mercury. "No Christmas tree EITHER? That means there's no Christmas left at all!"

"Perhaps we can go later today," Festus said as he stirred the breakfast porridge.

He didn't know what he could do to make Mercury happy. You could tell a mile away how upset the cat was—Mercury was standing in the corner stuffing carrots into the Christmas tree stand.

They ate breakfast in silence. They didn't even have any milk for their porridge.

Then there was a knock at the door, and Axel, the neighbor's son, peered into the kitchen.

"Merry Christmas, Festus," he said. "I came to help you clear the snow, but I see you've done it yourself."

Then he noticed the old man's brightly wrapped foot. Festus told him what had happened.

"Have you got enough food and wood and everything?" Axel asked.

"Well, we'll manage..." mumbled Festus.

At this, Mercury could not keep quiet any longer. He was hopping mad and sputtered, "We won't manage at all! We've got no food, only carrots, and no gingerbread and no Christmas tree, and I don't expect there'll be any Christmas presents either!"

"There, there, calm down," Festus shushed him. "We'll get by. But it would be good to have a drop of milk and some wood, perhaps, if you wouldn't mind..."

Axel stocked them up with a good supply of wood. Then he left, promising to come back soon with some milk.

Mercury was still unhappy. He shook the carrots out of the Christmas tree stand and tried to screw in a piece of wood.

"I think I know how to *make* a Christmas tree!" said Festus suddenly.

Festus told Mercury what to do. The cat ran outside and soon came back with the branches they had cut for the front door, along with a stick and a drill.

Festus drilled lots of holes in the stick. Then he screwed the stick into the Christmas tree stand, and he and Mercury carried everything into the parlor.

When they had put all the branches into the holes in the stick, it looked almost like a real Christmas tree.

"I wonder if that box of ornaments is under the bed," said Festus.

"You can wonder all you like, but that box is in the attic, and there it will stay," replied Mercury. "You can't get up there with that foot, and I can't open the door."

"I have another idea," said Festus. "Mercury, go to the workshop and see if you can find anything red or shiny, and I'll look around in here."

Festus hobbled around looking in drawers and cupboards. He found spoons, a clock, a thermometer, and a little metal monkey.

Mercury came back with a brush with red paint dried on it, a bike light, some springs, and other odds and ends.

Festus tied a piece of red thread to each new ornament, and Mercury hung them on the tree.

Then there was a knock at the kitchen door, and Axel came in with a little pail of milk and his mother, Elsa.

"Merry Christmas, Festus," said Elsa. "We've brought you some Christmas food. How's your foot?"

"It'll be all right, but you needn't have brought us any food. You're too kind," said Festus. But he took the basket anyway.

"Not at all. I'll put some coffee on, and you can treat me to some gingerbread. I've got some right here," said Elsa. And from her basket she pulled ham, meatballs, soup, doughnuts, and gingerbread.

Shortly afterward, Elsa's husband arrived. He said he wanted to borrow a hammer, but really he was curious about Festus's foot. He sat down with a cup of coffee to hear the whole story. Then old Mrs. Andersson came in.

"Merry Christmas, Festus," she said. "Elsa said you'd broken your leg and didn't have any food, so I thought I'd come over with a bit of sausage."

Festus bowed and thanked her and offered the old woman a seat.

"Mrs. Andersson's Christmas sausage is so good," declared Elsa, "I think I'll break my foot as well."

While they feasted, their neighbors the Lindgrens stopped by, and the kitchen was filled with the sounds of "Merry Christmas," chatter, and laughter. Mercury was forced to perform all his best tricks just to make them notice him at all.

Right after that, along came the Jonssons, and then the Nilssons' children, and they all had baskets with them because they had heard that Festus had broken his leg and was starving in his cottage, unable to move.

Mercury led the children into the parlor and showed them the tree. The ornaments were hung only as high as Mercury could reach, so the children helped him move them up.

"Come and see the tree!" the children called. "Mercury and Festus made it themselves."

Everyone crowded into the parlor and said, "It's a beautiful Christmas tree. You're a clever cat, Mercury."

Festus and Mercury thought so, too.

Soon it was dark and everyone had to go home. Their voices disappeared among the snowflakes. Although it was very quiet after they left, the excitement of the day still filled the little house.

Festus and Mercury lit the candles the children had made and put all the Christmas food they had been given on the table. Christmas Eve dinner was not usually such a splendid affair.

Then they went into the parlor and lit up the tree and gave each other their Christmas presents. Mercury got a yo-yo, and Festus got the potato peeler. They watched the fire burn down while they listened to Christmas carols. And Festus was happy.

"What a Christmas Eve it turned out to be, Mercury. We have such nice neighbors, don't you think?"

Mercury didn't answer, because he was fast asleep. He must have been happy too, though, because there was a smile on his face.

This edition first published 1989 by Carolrhoda Books, Inc.
Original edition copyright © 1988 by Sven Nordqvist
under the title PETTSON FÅR JULBESÖK.
English language rights arranged by Kerstin Kvint Literary
and Co-Production Agency, Stockholm, Sweden.

Library of Congress Cataloging-in-Publication Data

Nordqvist, Sven.
Merry Christmas, Festus and Mercury.

Translation of: Pettson får julbesök.
Summary: Unable to continue with Christmas preparations
because of his injured foot, old man Festus and his cat Mercury
face a bleak Christmas until the neighbors come to the rescue.
[1. Christmas—Fiction. 2. Old age—Fiction. 3. Cats—Fiction.
4. Neighborliness—Fiction] I. Title.
PZ7.N7756Me   1989   [E]   89-15766
ISBN 0-87614-383-4 (lib. bdg.)

Manufactured in the United States of America

1 2 3 4 5 6 7 8 9 10 98 97 96 95 94 93 92 91 90 89